WELCOME TO RYAN'S WORLD!

Ready-to-Read

Simon Spotlight

New York   London   Toronto   Sydney   New Delhi

SIMON SPOTLIGHT

An imprint of Simon & Schuster Children's Publishing Division
1230 Avenue of the Americas, New York, New York 10020
This Simon Spotlight edition July 2019
Text by May Nakamura

For information about special discounts for bulk purchases, please contact Simon & Schuster Special Sales at 1-866-506-1949 or business@simonandschuster.com.
Manufactured in the United States of America 1019 LAK
2 4 6 8 10 9 7 5 3
ISBN 978-1-5344-4077-7 (hc)
ISBN 978-1-5344-4076-0 (pbk)
ISBN 978-1-5344-4078-4 (eBook)

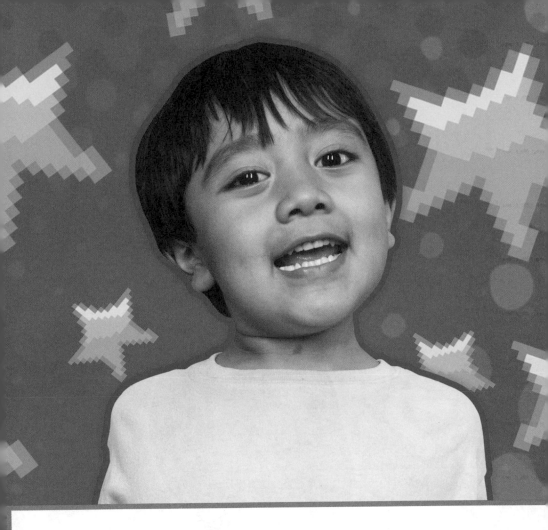

Hi, I am Ryan!

I am seven years old.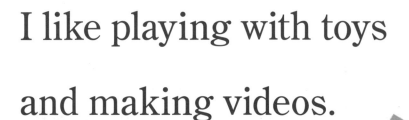

I like playing with toys

and making videos.

Have you ever heard of Ryan's World?

It is a place filled with all my favorite things!

Do you want to visit?

Follow me!

Now I am cartoon Ryan.

In my world, there are
so many ways to play!
We can play sports.
My favorite sports are
soccer and tennis.

I also like riding
my skateboard
and playing football.

We can drive around
like a race car driver.

We can also play
video games.
When I grow up,
I want to make
my own games!

In my world,

we can be anything.

We can pretend

to be pirates!

We can pretend to travel to space.

We can even be superheroes!

My superhero name

is Red Titan.

As Red Titan,

I am super strong!

I am getting hungry.

Let's eat pizza!

It is my favorite food.

Here is a whole pizza just for you!

What is your favorite pizza topping?

Now that we have eaten,

let's meet my friends.

This is Peck the penguin.

He likes science.

I do too!

This is Gus
the Gummy Gator.
He loves eating
yummy gummies.
Gus and his friend Moe
like exploring together.

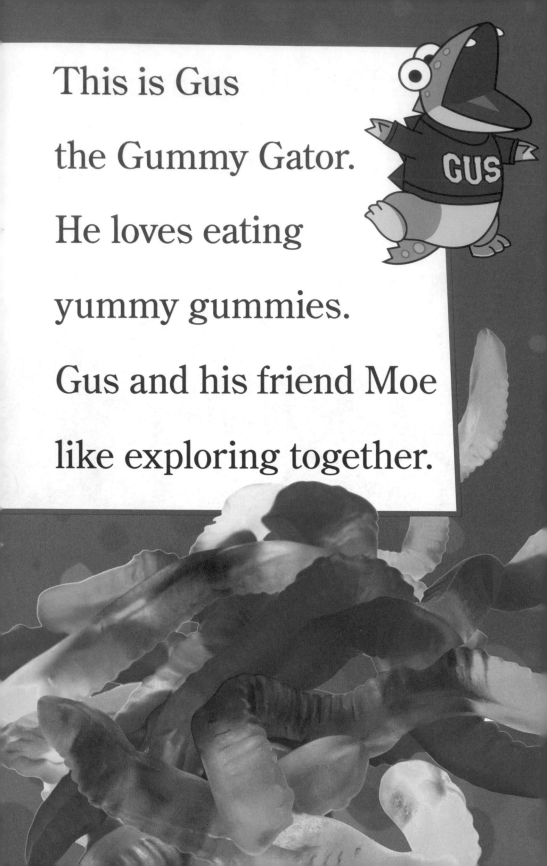

Once I ate the
largest gummy worm
in the world.
It was super sweet . . .
and yummy!

This is Alpha Lexa. She loves fashion and trying on new clothes.

Gil lives in the ocean.

He likes to swim with his

fish friends.

Combo Panda is not home.

I wonder where he is.

Look!

It is a mystery egg.

I like opening mystery eggs in my videos. What do you think is inside?

The egg is starting

to shake!

Wow!

Combo Panda

was hiding inside!

He is so silly!

I am glad you got to meet Combo Panda.

Now it is time to go home.

Thanks for visiting

Ryan's World!

Come visit me again soon!